RIDE FOR FREEDOM

The Story of Sybil Ludington

by Judy Hominick
and Jeanne Spreier

 Silver Moon Press
New York

First Silver Moon Press Edition 2001
Copyright © 2001 by Judy Hominick and Jeanne Spreier

The publisher would like to thank Everett Lee, historian of East Fishkill, New York,
for his historical direction and review. Special thanks also to Richard Muscarella, Putnam
County Historian, Minette Gunther and the other supremely helpful ladies of the Putnam
County Historical Society, and Steven Bates for his photography.

For information:
Silver Moon Press
New York, NY
(800) 874–3320

Library of Congress Cataloging-in-Publication Data
Hominick, Judy.
    Ride for freedom : the story of Sybil Ludington / by Judy Hominick and Jeanne
Spreier.-- 1st Silver Moon Press ed.
        p. cm. -- (Heroes to remember)
    Includes bibliographical references.
    Summary: In 1777, on a cold and stormy night in the New York Colony,
sixteen-year-old Sybil Ludington makes a dangerous and difficult ride to warn the local
militiamen that the British Army is looting and burning nearby Danbury, Connecticut.
    ISBN 1-893110-24-9
        1. Ludington, Sybil, b. 1761--Juvenile fiction. 2. United States--History--Revolution,
1775-1783--Juvenile fiction. 3. Danbury (Conn.)--History--Burning by the British,
1777--Juvenile fiction. [1. Ludington, Sybil, b. 1761--Fiction. 2. United
States--History--Revolution, 1775-1783--Fiction. 3. Danbury (Conn.)--History--Burning
by the British, 1777--Fiction.] I. Spreier, Jeanne. II. Title. III. Series.

PZ7.H74533 Ri 2001
[Fic]--dc21

                                                                              2001020832

Cover photograph and photographs on pages 8, 35, 41, 44, and 49 by Steven Bates.

Interior photographs courtesy of: the **Library of Congress**: page 7, page 12: LC-USZ62-1857, page 19: LC-D4-11613, page 22: LC-USZ62-102852; the **National Portrait Gallery**, Smithsonian Institution: page 5, NPG.77.23, oil on panel; The Collection of the **New-York Historical Society**: page 2: 74687, page 28: 40451; the **North Carolina Division of Archives and History**: page 25; the **Putnam County Historical Society** from *Colonel Henry Ludington: A Memoir*: page 8, page 44 (photographs by Steven Bates).

To my children,
Michael, Gary, Laurie, Stephen, and Melissa,
who are all extraordinary in their own special way.

J.H.

To Mary Lu, Wilson, and Joel,
who show me daily that young people do great things.

J.S.

One

Hooves pounded along the dirt path, breaking the early morning silence. Sybil crouched low on her horse, grasping the reins, her dress whipping behind her. She headed Star for the stream.

As she neared the water, she pulled up on the bay gelding, guiding him into the dense forest. "Good boy, Star. Slow and easy now. You know the way." Sybil patted Star's neck affectionately, as he carefully picked his way along the uneven path between towering trees.

Sybil reached again to her stocking, checking a third time for the message she had been asked to deliver. It was still safely hidden under her dress. Sybil felt a thrill to think that once again, a messenger from the Continental Army had arrived with a secret note for her to deliver. She really didn't know whom the note was originally from or who would finally receive the message. All she knew was that, at sixteen years old, she was doing her part to fight with the colonists against British rule. This wasn't the first time she had been asked to carry messages for the army.

The first time had been a year ago, when her father was home. He looked gravely at his oldest child, then just fifteen years old. "Sybil, what I'm asking you to do is very important," he had said.

A letter written by Henry Ludington to William Duer, Chairman of the Committee on Conspiracies of the Provincial Congress of the State of New York. The letter was sent from the township of Fredericksburgh where the Ludingtons lived and is dated December 3, 1776, only a few months before the events of this story *(Courtesy of the New-York Historical Society)*.

"Important and dangerous. If we weren't living in such desperate times, I would not ask it. Enoch Crosby must get this note—and no one else."

Sybil nodded. The young man spent many nights at the Ludington home in Fredericksburgh township. He always seemed to arrive mysteriously at night and was gone by dawn. Sybil wondered who he was, but she knew better than to ask her father, himself a colonel of the local militia regiment, about Enoch Crosby.

"Enoch's work is dangerous," her father said. "He pretends to be a Tory and works for the British Redcoats. He passes secret information to us through messengers. Sometimes, we need to get information back to Enoch. And we must pass those notes using someone who wouldn't be suspected of spying. Perhaps you could help."

Sybil could scarcely believe her ears. So that's what young Enoch did! Sybil knew she had been told a great secret. This was her chance to help in the war, a war many colonists were fighting against the British and their Tory loyalists in North America. The British wanted the colonies to remain under rule of the king. Sybil's father and others wanted to drive the British away. It was a cause that took her father away from home for months at a time.

She spoke before her father could say another word. "Father, I can do it! I know I can," Sybil pleaded. She wanted to be a part of the struggle against Britain. "Please say you'll let me. I promise I will be careful."

"All right, Sybil," he had said. "Your mother isn't

happy about this, but she knows 'tis the safest plan for our militia. You may go only in the daytime, though, never at night."

Sybil had been so frightened that first time. She thought every tree hid a Redcoat—that every person she passed knew the note was in her stocking.

Now, even after several trips over the past year, Sybil remained cautious.

A twig snapped ahead of Sybil. She immediately halted Star and hardly dared to breathe. Was someone there? She couldn't see clearly through the thicket. It would be impossible for Star to outrun a British spy in these woods if he stepped in front of her. Sybil looked for flashes of a red uniform among the dark tree trunks.

Birds tweeted happily. Some of the trees showed the green buds of spring, their limbs gently swaying in the moist breeze. Everything seemed so normal. Sybil took a deep breath and nudged Star on through the trees to the stream ahead.

Star walked into a clearing by the water. As always, Sybil looked around and saw no one. She dropped the reins, pretending she was doing nothing more than enjoying a ride in the woods. She let Star get a drink from the stream.

When she looked again behind her, a smiling Enoch Crosby stood there. She had not seen him in the woods, and she had not heard him as he stepped behind her.

"Hello, Sybil," the young spy said. "I've been expecting you."

Sybil bent down and pulled from her stocking the plain envelope with its red wax seal. Enoch took it from her. He slid the note into his vest.

"Thank you, Sybil. You are a brave girl. Best be on your way now. I will see you again." The young man turned and disappeared into the forest.

Sybil lifted Star's reins. "Let's go, Star. Our job is done for today."

An 1830 portrait of Enoch Crosby. By 1830 Enoch Crosby was famous for his role as a spy for the Continental Army during the Revolutionary War, some fifty years earlier. He claimed that his exploits as a young man were the basis for the popular novel, *The Spy*, by James Fenimore Cooper *(by Samuel Lovett Waldo and William Jewett, Courtesy of the National Portrait Gallery, Smithsonian Institution).*

Two

Sybil relaxed as she rode back through the woods. Signs of spring bloomed everywhere. Mayapples, with their umbrella-like leaves shading tiny white flowers, spotted the forest floor. Delicate lilies of the valley released their sweet scent, and by the roadsides, chicory plants, which Sybil's mother brewed into a tasty drink, were about to bloom bright blue.

But these were not happy times in the New York colony. In this year, 1777, life was anything but peaceful for colonists. Thousands of British soldiers were in the colonies to stop rebel action. In towns across the colonies, people had been ordered out of their homes by British soldiers. The soldiers lived in these private homes, forcing their owners either to leave and find refuge with sympathetic friends or relatives, or play host to the soldiers. Even the Ludingtons, who lived in the country, had been harassed by Redcoats, who came to their farm looking for food. Sybil's mother gave them chickens, flour, and salt, always in stony silence.

The rebels, including Sybil's father, believed the colonies should be free from English rule—no matter what the cost.

And what a cost it was to stay with England! The British taxed everything: newspapers, books, food coming into port, cotton going out. They took all the money they wanted from hardworking colonists without giving them a seat in England's Parliament. It was simply unfair.

A British tax stamp *(Courtesy of the Library of Congress)*.

Colonel Henry Ludington fought British troops and the Tories, who were British sympathizers living in America. As colonel of the militia in the Fredericksburgh Precinct, the Seventh Regiment of Dutchess County, Colonel Ludington's work paid off. The militia was so successful that the British had placed a reward of 300 English guineas for Colonel Ludington—captured dead or alive.

Shortly after the reward notice for Colonel Ludington was posted the year before, Sybil and her younger sister, Rebecca, spotted Tories hiding in the woods near their home. The girls had been outside standing watch, muskets resting against their shoulders, while their father was inside preparing to leave once again.

This document gave Colonel Ludington a position of command over the Seventh Regiment of the Dutchess County militia. He was commissioned as a colonel by the Provincial Congress for the Colony of New York, June 1776 *(Courtesy of the Putnam County Historical Society)*.

"Rebecca," Sybil whispered, "men are hiding behind those trees."

"You think they're Tories?" Rebecca whispered back, trying not to look.

"Of course. They'd do anything for the reward money," Sybil answered. "Walk calmly into the house to warn Father. Don't run. They can't know we've seen them." Rebecca strolled inside. In a few minutes Sybil followed her. The girls quickly lit candles and put them in all the windows, hoping it would appear that there were lots of people visiting the Ludingtons that evening.

"Now, everyone walk back and forth in front of the windows," Colonel Ludington directed his wife and children. Throughout the evening, the Ludingtons moved about the house, knowing Tories watched from the woods.

No one came and no one left their home, but it certainly looked as if many people were inside. All night, the Tories waited in the woods. All night, the Ludingtons kept moving, giving the appearance that people filled their house.

Sybil's family was exhausted by daybreak, but the Tories were exhausted and confused! By dawn, they gave up their vigil and left the woods.

*   *   *

Star snorted, bringing Sybil out of her reverie. She patted him, staring at the dark branches that sliced the morning sunlight into shadows. Now, Colonel Ludington was gone again. Even in winter, the Ludingtons were busy doing work normally done by farmers. The family all helped make maple syrup throughout March, hanging buckets on maple trees in the woods near their home, then collecting them once they filled with sap.

It was exhausting work with little to show for it. Sybil had carefully placed the sap buckets on a sled, which she and her brothers pulled along icy tracks back to the farm's cookhouse. Sybil figured they hauled eighty gallons of sap from the woods this year. Mother poured it into a huge iron kettle, hung above a wood fire. From each forty gallons of sap they collected, the family could expect to get about a gallon of pure maple syrup. In the frosty weather, it seemed like a lot of cold, difficult work for such little payback, but Sybil knew nothing tasted better on biscuits than rich, sweet maple syrup.

As Sybil neared her home, she could see a wisp of smoke curling from the chimney of the keeping room. *Mother will be fixing the noontime meal,* Sybil thought. *Biscuits and syrup—that will taste good. I should hurry and help her.*

Sybil noticed right away something was different about the house. It gave her an uneasy feeling, and she prodded Star into a trot.

Then it struck her. Not one of her seven brothers and sisters was outside. Everyone seemed to be gone.

Sybil hurriedly dismounted. Had something happened to her family while she was away?

Three

Sybil's heart pounded as she reached the house. She quickly tied Star to a fence post. Across the yard was a scrawny horse she'd never seen before. *Hmm*, thought Sybil, *I wonder who's visiting.* Then it struck her. It was Colonel Ludington's mare that stood nearby, thinner and weaker than two months ago, when Sybil saw her last. The mare eagerly pushed her nose into a bucket at her feet, no doubt containing a portion of oats.

Father was back!

Sybil raced inside, throwing open the door and not even worrying to close it.

"Father!" she shouted.

"Ay, my girl!" Henry Ludington called back, rushing forward to grab her in a hug. "I hear you've been busy this morning. Already been riding through the woods and enjoying the fresh water in the stream, I see." He gave her a broad smile, a sly wink, and a squeeze on the cheek.

"Yes," Sybil smiled back. "Mother sent me out for fresh air this morning. The weather just begs we take note of it."

"Was it enjoyable, then?" her father asked.

"It was a most successful ride," Sybil answered. She, her mother, and father all smiled, sharing the secret among them.

"Well, then, let's eat!" Colonel Ludington boomed. "I haven't had one of my wife's delicious meals in a very long time. And, I hear," he said, looking at all the children, "we've a special treat today because of all your hard work. Syrup with my biscuits today, is it? Well done, well done!"

A New England kitchen during the colonial era. The Ludington kitchen may have looked something like this *(Courtesy of the Library of Congress)*.

✳   ✳   ✳

That night was pitch black as low clouds rolled in, covering the moon and stars above. About twenty miles away from the Ludington's house, near the small New York village of Red Mills,* one of the colonel's friends and fellow freedom fighters was also enjoying his first night at home in many weeks. Mr. Hasbrouck finished his hot evening meal and warm conversation with his wife and family, before preparing for bed.

In the woods a hundred yards away, four men were hiding.

"I believe the old man is to bed," one of the gruff men whispered.

"Looks like the lights are out, for sure," another muttered.

"You two stay here. Ben and I will go get those horses now," the leader ordered.

Two men dressed in dark clothes carefully stepped out of the woods behind the Hasbroucks' farmhouse. With no moon to cast a shadow, it was easy for them to walk unseen to the barn. They stopped by the barn door, looking back to make sure the lights were out in the Hasbroucks' house.

"Come on, let's go," the leader said.

He opened the barn door.

SCREECH!

"Blasted door!" he muttered. "Quick, get in."

The two slid into the barn. Immediately chickens inside started scurrying about and clucking. A goose began to honk.

"Oh blast! Let's get going," the leader hissed as he lit a candle. The two men didn't speak. Each knew exactly what to do. The second man grabbed two harnesses off the wall and jumped into the stall. He quickly slid the bit into one horse's mouth and pulled the leather straps up over the horse's ears. In a flash he secured the buckles. He stepped over to the next horse and did the same. Within a minute he was astride the second horse.

The other man carefully set down the candle, slid open the bolt holding the door of the stall shut, and grabbed the reins of the first horse, flinging his leg over the horse's back.

"Let's get out of here!" the leader shouted as he dug his heels into the horse's ribs.

"The barn door—it's not open!" his partner yelled.

"No time—let's go!"

The horses charged forward, pushing against the door. The leather hinges ripped as the door banged against the barn.

A bright light shone in the yard.

"Who's that!" It was Mr. Hasbrouck, holding his lantern aloft.

"Stop, you Skinner thieves!" Mr. Hasbrouck yelled as the two horses galloped past. "You evil Skinners—no loyalty except to money!" He wheeled around, running back to the open door of his house, where his wife stood.

"Get out of my way!" he yelled. "I need my musket."

"Dear, they're gone and surely there are more of

them in the woods. You'll never be able to get the horses back," Mrs. Hasbrouck said, trying to calm her husband. "Worse yet, you might get hurt and then where would we be?"

"I suppose those Skinners had an order for horses from the Redcoats. The British are probably paying them off now, and my precious horses will be fighting for the king. This war's tearing us up, dear, and I feel like there's nothing I can do."

$\mathcal{F}our$

"At least two of them, maybe more," Mr. Hasbrouck reported the next day to Colonel Ludington. "It was so dark I couldn't get a good look at 'em. We had just retired for the night when I heard my chickens unsettled. And then the goose started honking. That's a bad sign, ye know."

"Ay, ay, 'tis for sure," the colonel agreed.

"I ran outside with my lantern. And here these two fellows just charge past me—galloping they were. They ripped the barn door clear off two hinges. I'll need to repair that as soon as I get back.

"These fellows, they must have known me," Mr. Hasbrouck continued. "They got in the barn right quick, knew just where I keep the harnesses and had the horses out in the wink of an eye."

"Skinners, you suppose?" Colonel Ludington asked.

"Of course they were Skinners!" Mr. Hasbrouck barked. "Who else would steal a man's horse? Loyalty to no one, those outlaws. All they care about is the money they get from the British army when they deliver their stolen goods. I had to borrow me neighbor's mule to get here this morning and tell you what's happening in our part of the country. Why just the other day, Mrs. Hasbrouck tells me, neighbors had five hams stolen from their smokehouse during the night. It's a good thing spring's here and they won't need preserved food. But imagine! Five hams! That's not to feed your hungry family—that's to sell to those conniving Redcoats."

"It's not good, that's the truth," Colonel Ludington agreed. "Too bad you didn't see who they were. We could put an end to this stealing and treachery once and for all if we knew who was behind it."

"To carry five hams you'd need at least three with horses," Mr. Hasbrouck said. "But surely there's more thieves than that."

Sybil set a mug of buttermilk in front of each man. "Thank you kindly, young lady," Mr. Hasbrouck said. "Even with this ill news, it's good to be in your home again."

"It worries me, Mr. Hasbrouck, that these Skinners are moving farther out into the country, terrorizing homes we thought were safe," Colonel Ludington said.

"Ay, I truly believed my missus was fine at the home while I was gone, but now I'm not so sure," the farmer replied, his voice barely a whisper. "I tell you, Colonel, it worries me that the Redcoats are moving inland. I fear for Danbury, I fear we've too much to lose in that town."

"Sybil, please come help me."

The voice of Mrs. Ludington startled Sybil, who had been straining to hear the men's conversation.

"Sybil," Mrs. Ludington repeated. "We need to fetch the ashes from the barn so we can get to making soap."

Oh, drat! Sybil hated making soap more than anything else. Everything about it was hot, dirty, difficult, and boring. Sybil turned to her mother.

"Please, mother, can we do this tomorrow?"

"Sybil, now," her mother replied.

Sybil reluctantly left the kitchen and traipsed to the barn. She hoisted one of the bushel baskets filled with ash, which was collected every morning before her mother built up the kitchen fire for the day's cooking. Nine other bushel baskets, similarly filled with cold ashes, stood waiting nearby. Rebecca joined her sister in the barn. She picked up a bucket of lime.

"I don't see why the boys can't do this," Rebecca complained to her sister.

"I guess they're just too young. Mother didn't have us make soap until we were ten years old. And remember that time lye splashed on my hand, it burned for days," Sybil said.

The girls carried their dirty loads outside to a large barrel sitting on top of a wooden frame in the farmyard. Their mother had already placed an earthen jug under the barrel, where a hole had been drilled in its bottom. She then added a layer of straw in the barrel. Sybil upended her basket into the barrel, the soot flying in the air and covering her face. She started to cough.

Rebecca added a layer of lime on top of the ashes. The girls both filled pails with water from a nearby rain barrel.

"Why can't we wait until Mr. Hasbrouck leaves before we start this?" Sybil asked her mother, who made sure the lye water dripping through the bottom

A Pennsylvania woman making soap. Although this picture was taken in 1900, it shows that soap making in rural life hadn't changed much in 120 years *(Courtesy of the Library of Congress)*.

was being collected in the jug.

"We're short on soap," Mrs. Ludington replied. "If your father has to leave tonight, he'll take the last of what we have. I'm sorry, but this chore can't wait."

"Mother, this is going to take all day. Why can't one of the boys at least come out while the soap is boiling so I can go in with Father and Mr. Hasbrouck?" Sybil asked.

"We mustn't bother your father and Mr. Hasbrouck while they talk about army business," she replied. "This isn't the sort of thing you need to worry about. But Sybil," she continued, "you do need to know that things are getting dangerous. Very dangerous. It isn't for fun that we send you to meet Mr. Crosby. It's serious business."

Sybil and Rebecca stood in stony silence. The war was real. Many brave people died fighting for the cause. One day, it could be one of them.

Five

Sybil and Rebecca dragged themselves through the back door for supper. Soot covered the girls from head to toe. Despite the cool spring weather, they were sweaty from stoking the fire that burned for hours under the soap pot, while they stirred the sludge of lye water and fat until it thickened. Finally the girls had poured the mixture into barrels and headed into the house.

A huge stone fireplace covered the wall of the keeping room. Mrs. Ludington was getting the smaller children to bed upstairs.

Stew simmered in a pot hanging above the fire. On the table was a pan of half-eaten cornbread, cold now because Mrs. Ludington had baked it for the evening meal. Most of the family had eaten hours ago. Sybil and Rebecca, the last to eat that evening, poured themselves glasses of milk, cut large hunks of bread, and scooped some of the hearty stew onto their plates.

"I don't know if I can eat, I'm so tired," Rebecca said.

"I wonder what father and Mr. Hasbrouck were talking about," Sybil said, her mind still turning over the few comments she'd heard earlier that day. "I wonder why they were worried about Danbury."

A 1776 farmhouse. In addition to soap making, Sybil and Rebecca's daily chores would probably have included spinning flax on a spinning wheel like the one shown here *(Courtesy of the Library of Congress)*.

"All the army supplies are there—maybe Father is worried about that," Rebecca said.

"But the supplies are safe, right?" Sybil asked, more to herself than to her sister. "Connecticut's Gallant Seventeen are there guarding those supplies. And the British, they're here in New York, so why would Mr. Hasbrouck worry about Danbury?"

"Sybil, that Connecticut regiment can't be very big," Rebecca said. "Besides, New York and Connecticut are next to each other. If the British are here in New York, they could be in Connecticut in a day."

"But no British troops are in that area. I just can't figure why they're concerned," Sybil commented.

"Sybil, Rebecca," their mother entered the room. "You girls need to finish supper and get washed up. You look like you rolled in ashes."

"We feel like we rolled in ashes," Rebecca said. "I, for one, can't wait to crawl into my bed. I'll be done in a few minutes, Momma."

Sybil pulled a pickle from a crock stored under the table. "I'm almost done, too," she said, munching her pickle and carrying her plate and mug to the washbasin. "I plan to sleep well past dawn tomorrow."

*   *   *

Seventeen miles east of the Ludington's New York farm, orange and red flames licked the skies of Danbury, Connecticut. Most residents had fled as British soldiers marched into town the day before. Now, soldiers ran through the streets, smashing windows with their muskets. The tinkle of glass mixed with the sounds of drunken soldiers yelling to one another as they shot off cannons down the streets.

Redcoats broke open doors to stores and taverns, dragging barrels outside.

"That'll teach these colonists!" one soldier yelled as he hacked open a barrel of corn syrup, allowing the precious liquid to spill down the cobblestone street.

"These colonists think they can whip us!" shouted another. "Let's just see them beat us without their precious supplies!" He held a burning torch aloft and touched it to the corner of a wooden storage barn. In just a few minutes, flames dashed along the bottom boards of the barn. Soon, the entire building was ablaze. The house next door caught fire, too.

In the next block, soldiers walked from house to house, looking for a cross on the front. Those were the homes of Tories, who supported British soldiers. The houses without a cross were set on fire. British soldiers cheered as each house became a huge bonfire.

Sounds of destruction filled the streets of Danbury, but almost no one, other than the British soldiers, were there to see the chaos. Most of the militia soldiers, in Danbury just a few weeks before, had gone home to start planting. Danbury, with its vast stores of medical and military supplies and food to help the Continental Army in its fight for freedom, was left unprotected. Now, two thousand British soldiers rampaged through the town.

Soldiers swaggered through town, drinking rum

and wine from the kegs they had stolen. The soldiers' leader, General William Tryon, stayed at the army headquarters set up in a Tory house. He didn't really know what was going on outside in Danbury's streets.

And he didn't really care.

General William Tryon. Henry Ludington had once served in the militia under General Tryon, but when the Americans proclaimed independence, the colonel was forced to fight against his former commanding officer *(Courtesy of the North Carolina Division for Archives and History).*

Six

Rain moved in that evening. For the Ludingtons, the patter of raindrops on the roof over their heads sounded like a nighttime lullaby. The children snuggled into their feather beds, covered by quilts Mrs. Ludington so diligently pieced each winter evening. The next day, everyone knew, would bring just as much work as today. Everyone slept soundly.

Bang, bang, bang!

"Colonel Ludington, Colonel Ludington!"

Bang, bang, bang!

"Good gracious, who in the world could that be, Henry?" Mrs. Ludington said. She nudged her husband, who slept through the noise.

"Colonel Ludington!"

The voice from below was louder. Sybil popped her head into her parents' bedroom.

"Father! Someone is outside asking for you. Should I let him in?"

"NO! Sybil you stay here." Her father was fully awake, climbing from his bed and into his breeches. He lit a candle and walked quietly down the stairs.

Sybil and her mother walked to the top of the dark staircase and listened to the conversation below.

"Who are you?" the colonel yelled through the door.

The women couldn't hear the muffled reply.

"How do I know you are who you say?" the colonel responded.

Again, the women couldn't hear the response.

"All right, all right, just a minute." The women heard the door bolt slide back. They walked partway down the stairs to see who entered.

A young man stepped inside. "Thank you, sir," he said. Mrs. Ludington came down the stairs. "I'm sorry, Mrs. Ludington, to wake you up this rainy night. But it's horrible news. Danbury is lost, completely lost!"

"Henry, why don't you take this young man to the keeping room. Sybil, get this man some dry clothes from your father's cabinet." Mrs. Ludington took the candle from her husband and lit another in the hall. They walked to the keeping room where the colonel built up the smoldering fire.

Sybil ran in, almost breathless, carrying dry trousers and a shirt.

"What's going on?" she asked. "What's happening in Danbury?"

"He says the British set the city afire. No one was

left to protect the Continental Army's supplies. Most of the militia had gone back to their homes to plant. Now the people who had stayed in the city have fled," Colonel Ludington answered, while the young man slipped out into the hall to change into dry clothes.

"Sir, it's worse than that," the young man said, reemerging in the colonel's oversized, but dry, clothes. "The British say they will kill all the young boys so none will grow up to be soldiers. When the Redcoats marched through Red Mills on their way to Danbury, people fled to the woods. One poor woman had sick children and was forced to stay

A 1777 silhouette of Colonel Henry Ludington *(Courtesy of the New-York Historical Society)*.

behind. She was so scared to be alone in town with her ill children."

"Did she survive?" Mrs. Ludington asked with a quivering voice.

"Yes, ma'am, she did. But can you think how frightened that poor woman was as those Redcoats marched through?" the messenger answered.

"When did they get to Danbury?" Colonel Ludington asked.

"Yesterday, sir. It was bad enough last night. They were a loud and unruly group. They shot cannons down the street and stole rum from taverns around town. It appears they started again today to loot shops and taverns. We need help in Danbury, sir. Others have gone to muster troops in nearby towns, but we need all the help we can get."

"Of course, of course," the colonel answered. "I'll gather my men as quickly as possible. We were afraid for Danbury—and now I see with good cause. Dear Abigail, could you get this young man some food and start preparing my pack?" He turned to the young man sitting at the table. "You can't continue this journey. Obviously you don't know this country."

"Father, what about me? I know my way," Sybil said.

"Archie is too young," her father said, ignoring Sybil. "I must stay here and prepare for the march to Danbury. Abigail, we'll need food for the men as they muster here."

"Father, I can go!" Sybil tugged at her father's sleeve. "I know where your men live. Star is such a good horse, he practically knows his own way."

"Oh, Sybil," her mother said. "It's dark and raining. There are Skinners out."

"But mother, who else is there? Father can't go. He must organize the men when they come. Archie is just nine years old and this poor young man is spent. I can go! I've been carrying messages for months now."

"Yes, but only during the day," her mother said.

"Abigail, who do we send if we don't send Sybil?" her father asked. "Skinners won't be out on a night like this. It's too miserable even for them. Sybil, go back to my dresser. Find a pair of breeches, a shirt, and a vest. Abigail, we'll have to prepare a pack for her. It's a long ride. Sybil, this is your night to help the revolution. Go get ready."

$\mathcal{S}$even

Sybil clumped down the stairs in her work boots. "Father, I'm ready to go," she said as she entered the keeping room. She wore breeches tucked into the boots, a flannel shirt, a vest over that, and her own heavy coat. The spring rain made it a cold night.

"Not so fast, please, Sybil," her mother said. "Come here and let me plait your hair. You can't go off in the woods with your hair flying behind you."

Sybil sat down before her mother.

"You must go to Shaw's Pond* and then take the road to Mahopac," her father said. "That will be fairly safe, too, and you should have no trouble. Next is the long road to Red Mills and the Hasbrouck house after that. You must watch carefully for Tories who patrol the roads around Red Mills."

"Sybil, you should make a stop at the Hasbroucks'. Take a break there," her mother said. "I know Mrs.

*Now called Carmel.

Hasbrouck will welcome you inside for a few minutes."

"It's a good place to stop," the colonel agreed, "because by then you'll have made it by Tory sympathizers who live near there. You need to be vigilant—watch for lanterns in the woods that would give them away.

"The roads will be muddy and slippery—dangerous even without the Tories. Sybil, don't take the time to dismount," her father continued. "Just rap on the windows with a stick and tell the men to muster at Ludington Mill.

"After you leave Hasbroucks', stay on the road to Stormville and then take the road to Pecksville and on home.

"Let's see," the colonel said, "the trip should be about forty miles, I would guess. That's a bit of territory. You'll have to keep your eyes open for Skinner fires out in the woods—although on a night like this, I suspect they won't be up to much trouble. But if you see any, stay clear. Whatever you do, don't get off Star. As long as you're on horseback, you'll have the upper hand."

Mrs. Ludington tied strings around the ends of Sybil's braids and handed a saddlebag to her sixteen-year-old daughter. "Here's some food."

"Mother, I'll be fine. I know these roads well. Come help me get Star ready for the trip."

Sybil and her mother walked out together, leaving the two men alone.

"Sir, how will she make the ride? She's so young," the messenger asked Colonel Ludington.

"Son, that girl is a brave and valiant fighter for the revolution. She'll do just fine."

*   *   *

Star snorted as Sybil and her mother, carrying a lantern, entered the stall. Sybil threw a blanket across the horse's back, followed by her father's saddle. She buckled the girth and adjusted the stirrup leathers. She slipped the simple halter onto Star's head.

Colonel Ludington walked into the stall and started checking the buckles on Star's saddle. "Everything looks good, ladies," he said. He handed his daughter a stick. "Use this to bang on windows," he instructed Sybil. Then he and Mrs. Ludington led the horse out of the barn into the gloomy night.

The lantern cast long shadows across the barnyard as the two parents watched their daughter prepare to leave. "Godspeed," Sybil's mother said simply. Her father gave Star a slap on the rump.

"Mother, Father, I love you. I'll be back," Sybil called over her shoulder as she headed off into the drizzling darkness.

$\mathcal{E}ight$

"**M**uster at Ludingtons'! Danbury is burning! Hurry!" Sybil rapped on a window at the Mahopac crossroads with her stick.

A man poked his head out of the door.

"Who's there in this rain?" he called.

"It's me, Sybil Ludington. Look at the sky. Can you see? The British are burning Danbury." Sybil steered Star over to the next house and banged on the window. A light moved to the window and a man stepped outside. "Hurry!" she told him, "Gather your gear. Muster at Ludington's Mill! Danbury is burning. I've been to Shaw's Pond already. Tell the others nearby. We must move quickly."

She spun Star in the mud, cantering back to the narrow road and heading for her next stop, to the north. Her wool clothes, damp from the drizzle, clung to her arms and legs. The cold chilled her to the bone.

She headed north. No houses along this road, she knew. Clouds blocked the moonlight. Thick woods crowded the road. And this was where Skinners were known to camp, hidden among the trees. They'd think nothing of stopping her and stealing her fine gelding. Sybil knew she'd have to be careful along these next twelve miles.

Star could only walk along the winding, muddy road. Tree branches, felled during the day's storm, blocked her path in places.

"Star, this is going to be a long trip. It's going to take us almost three hours to get to Red Mills. You'll have to watch with me, Star. You need to make sure we see the Skinners before they see us."

Star picked his way along the road. Sybil moved her head from side to side, trying to look in the woods for signs of robbers.

A road sign marking the route Sybil took on the night of April 26, 1777 *(photograph by Steven Bates)*.

"OUCH!" Sybil screamed. She felt a wet sting on her face. Her heart raced until she realized it was a branch that had slapped her. She felt the warm trickle of blood down her cheek.

I need to be calm, Sybil told herself. *I need to keep my wits about me. Don't borrow trouble.*

She gave Star a pat on the neck and kept going.

*   *   *

Honk, honk, honk!

Sybil pulled back on the reins. Honk, Honk!

Could she be near Red Mills? With no moon or stars in the sky it had been impossible to keep track of time. "Whoa, Star," Sybil whispered. "It sounds like we're coming up to some houses." She peered through the darkness to see if she could make out the shapes of buildings.

Sybil shivered in her wet clothes. She was tired and more than anything wanted something warm to drink. *Tea would be very good right now,* she thought. She nudged Star forward a few steps then stopped again. The scent of burning wood wafted through the air.

"Houses for sure," Sybil whispered to Star. "We need to be quick about this—but quiet."

She and Star moved forward around a bend in the road. Ahead, she could make out the faint glow of light in a window. Her heart raced. If she alerted the wrong house, she would tip off the Tories living in the town.

Star snorted. "Shh," Sybil hissed at her horse.

"Please, Star, be quiet." Geese honked again. Sybil felt as if her heart were pounding too loudly.

"We need to get to just one house on the north side of town," Sybil said to calm herself. "Oh, those blasted geese. If only they'd be quiet."

By now she could make out a few houses that lined the road through town. She knew a militiaman lived in the last house. Should she go right up the road or try to circle round the back?

Sybil decided to ride right through the village and take her chances. If someone came out, she'd simply spur Star on and race through town.

She passed the first house, then the second. Nothing happened. Sybil relaxed a bit. Finally, she reached the militiaman's house and quietly knocked on a window.

"Who's out there?" A voice boomed through the window.

Nine

"Shh, sir," Sybil whispered as loud as she dared. "Please help me." Sybil heard the door bolt slide open. The door opened a crack.

"What do you need?" the man's voice boomed again.

"Sir, it's Sybil Ludington," she answered quietly.

"Oh! The colonel's daughter! Why didn't you say so?" The man immediately dropped his voice to a whisper. "Do you have news?"

Sybil felt relief wash across her as she realized she had knocked at the right house. This was a militiaman who knew her father.

"Quickly, sir, the troops are mustering at Ludington Mill. The British have burned Danbury. My father needs help."

"Young lady, come in. You're wet and tired. My wife will take care of you," he answered.

"No sir, I must gather more men," Sybil was already heading Star on the road north.

"How far do you have to go, girl?" the man asked.

"I'm about half-way through," Sybil called over her shoulder. She didn't hear the man's next question. She was intent on reaching the Hasbroucks' house, her next stop.

*   *   *

Rain started falling again as Sybil rode to the Hasbroucks'. Sybil judged she'd been riding almost five hours, not once getting off her horse. Her wet clothes rubbed her cold skin raw, and she knew her face and hands must be bloody with thousands of little scratches she got from riding along the narrow trail. She wanted to push Star into a canter, but she knew the roads were too thick with mud to take that chance.

What was that? "Whoa, Star," Sybil whispered, listening as hard as she could. It sounded like voices.

Sybil headed Star into the woods, cringing as her horse snapped sticks and slogged through wet leaves. *The noise will surely give us away*, she thought. She ducked low in the saddle, trying to avoid branches as they whipped by. She stopped, petting Star to soothe him.

Two men on horseback, talking loudly and laughing as if it were a sunny day, rode by just a minute later. One of them carried a lantern. Sybil could tell these were Skinners. A ham hung from each man's saddle, and an extra saddle was strapped to each man's horse. *They've just robbed a farm,* Sybil thought, *and I can't do anything about it.*

In just a moment, they disappeared around a bend in the road. Sybil waited in the woods, as rain poured over her head and dripped down her back. After counting to three hundred, she carefully made her way back to the road. She was even more determined to get to the Hasbroucks' house now.

*   *   *

It was about three o'clock in the morning, but to Sybil it felt like sunrise. She prodded Star into a canter as she approached the Hasbroucks' house. With her stout stick, she started rapping the front window.

"Mr. Hasbrouck! Mr. Hasbrouck!" she yelled.

An upstairs window screeched open. "Who's down there at this hour?" Mr. Hasbrouck's voice boomed.

"It's me, Sybil," she yelled back. "Danbury's burning. Father's mustering troops at our house. You must get the others nearby quickly and go help."

A woman's head appeared at the window. "Sybil Ludington, you get off that horse and come inside."

"Gladly Mrs. Hasbrouck," the girl responded. "Gladly."

She almost fell off Star's back, her legs were so cold and numb. By this time, Mr. Hasbrouck was downstairs, hitching up his breeches and coming outside to help her. "My dear girl," he said as he reached Sybil's side with his lantern, "you look like you've been in a fight."

Waiting at the door was his wife. "Inside right now, Sybil. I can't believe the state you're in." Sybil happily followed orders, letting the warmth and safety of the house envelop her.

Mrs. Hasbrouck held flannel cloths and dry shirts and trousers in her arms. She helped Sybil peel the layers of wet clothes off and wrapped her in flannel to dry her off. "Sit here," she told Sybil, "while I dry your hair. Oh my goodness. Your face. Your mother wouldn't recognize you." She placed a kettle of water over the fire. Mrs. Hasbrouck poured warm water into a bowl, dipped a cloth into the water, and cleaned the scratches marking Sybil's face and arms.

The Hasbrouck House as it appears today *(photograph by Steven Bates).*

Mr. Hasbrouck stomped into the room. "Star's taken care of. That horse is tired, young lady. He needs to rest too."

"I must get to Stormville," Sybil protested.

"Where have you been?" Mr. Hasbrouck asked.

Sybil recounted her journey including the near meeting with two Skinners. "I must get to the men in Stormville and Pecksville," Sybil ended. "My father needs their help."

"I'll take a different route to your house and wake up men along the way," Mr. Hasbrouck said. "You, dear girl, must get a mug of something hot to drink and some food in your belly before you leave again."

"Your mother would never forgive me if I let you get back on that horse without a good meal," Mrs. Hasbrouck agreed, placing sliced cornmeal mush and bacon in a skillet for her husband and Sybil. "I'll fry this quickly, and you can both be on your way."

Ten

The rain had moved west and dawn did little to brighten the gray sky. As Sybil neared her family's house, she met men and horses on the way to muster with others. The long, lonely, and dangerous ride was nearing its end.

"Hey, here's the girl," a man called out as Sybil trotted up on Star's back. "Make way for the Ludington girl!"

Men ahead of her moved to the side of the road. Bone tired and wearing the ill-fitting clothes she borrowed from the Hasbroucks, Sybil gave a weak smile. She moved toward her house.

In the farmyard, almost four hundred men, many with horses, stood waiting for the last militiamen to join them. "It's Sybil!" one of the men yelled out.

Sybil heard her father's deep voice boom above the noise of men talking. "Sybil, Sybil! Where are you?" Mr. Ludington came running toward the road. Sybil halted Star and stood quietly until her father reached her. "Sybil, you're here. You're safe. Oh my, child. You look weary. Here, off that horse. Let's get inside."

Sybil's brother Archie had followed Colonel Ludington to greet her. "Quick, son, get a blanket for me. Sybil, get down. You're home now," her father said.

"Father, did everyone get here? Can they save Danbury?"

"Sybil, just look around at all the men here. This is because of you," her father said.

Archie ran up with a blanket and threw it around his sister's shoulders. "Sybil, I'll take Star now," he said kindly. "You need to rest."

The Ludington mill, where the troops mustered that morning of April 27, 1777. The Ludington mill stood until 1972 when it was destroyed by fire *(Courtesy of the Putnam County Historical Society)*.

"And you need to eat and get some fresh clothes on and not worry anymore. Let's get through this crowd and into the house." Colonel Ludington gently steered his tired daughter through the crowds of men waiting for the word to move out toward Danbury.

Mrs. Ludington came running down the path from the house. She gathered Sybil in her arms.

"Look, it's the girl!" a man yelled, as Sybil trudged by with a parent on either side. He started clapping. In seconds, all the men in his group started clapping. Men in the next group took up the clapping and started cheering for the young woman. Soon, all the men gathered in the yard were cheering, clapping, and stomping their feet.

Despite the clouds, Sybil knew it was going to be a great day of victory.

Postscript

Sybil started her ride on Saturday night and arrived home Sunday morning, along with militiamen under her father's command. That Sunday, the British general in Danbury, William Tryon, was warned that the colonists were on their way to the town. He fled with his troops early in the day. When the British troops realized they couldn't carry Continental Army supplies with them as they retreated, they destroyed what they could. Carrying the supplies would have made the retreating British army vulnerable to militia attack.

Colonel Henry Ludington's troops, about four hundred strong, as well as others in the area, marched into Danbury on Sunday afternoon. The town lay in shambles. Homes and businesses had been burned or destroyed.

Sybil's ride had far-reaching results. She roused the militiamen who were able to save their own homes and those of their New York neighbors and friends. And while Colonel Ludington and other colonists failed to save Danbury, they did thwart General Tryon's plans to march farther inland and capture territory in Dutchess and Westchester counties.

While sixteen-year-old Sybil Ludington's forty-mile-ride through a rain-soaked countryside blanketed with woods has remained largely unknown throughout the years, the midnight ride of Paul Revere, a forty-year-old Boston silversmith, was made famous in Henry

Stamp created in 1975 to honor Sybil Ludington.

Wadsworth Longfellow's 1861 poem, "Paul Revere's Ride." In April 1775, Paul Revere rode twelve miles on well-traveled roads from Boston to Concord, Massachusetts, to tell minutemen that British regulars were on the move. Longfellow's poem leaves out critical details, including that Revere rode with two others for much of the time (although he was alone for a brief portion of the journey) and that he was captured by six Redcoats and held for several hours.

Like Sybil Ludington, who rode two years later, one of Revere's most important contributions was to energize colonists in their fight for freedom. The bravery of both riders inspired people to take up arms against the British, despite the odds against them.

The statue of Sybil Ludington that stands on the shores of Lake Mahopac in Carmel, New York (*photograph by Steven Bates*).

Sybil married Edmond Ogden when she was twenty-three years old. They had one child, Henry. Her husband died, possibly of yellow fever, in 1799.

In 1804, when Henry was eighteen years old, Sybil opened a tavern to help support herself and her son. Even though she was a widow, Sybil paid for Henry to attend law school. He married and had six children.

Sybil's descendants continued to play an important role in building the nation. One of Henry's sons, Edmund Augustus Ogden had a distinguished career in the army, leading troops in the Blackhawk and Mexican Wars. He constructed Fort Riley in the Kansas Territories, and after he died there of cholera in 1855, a plaque was erected in his honor.

In 1961 the Daughters of the American Revolution erected a statue of Sybil sculpted by Anna Leah Huntington in Carmel, New York, and in

Sybil Ludington's gravestone in Patterson, New York *(photograph by Steven Bates).*

Postscript

1975 a U.S. postage stamp was created in her honor. Throughout Putnam County, signs mark the path of her brave ride on that stormy night in 1777. Over her grave and that of her father in the Patterson Baptist Church cemetery, there is a plaque commemorating them as heroes of the American Revolution.

Selected Bibliography

Bailey, James Montgomery. *History of Danbury, Connecticut 1684-1896*. New York: Burr Printing House, 1896.

Barrett, Tracy. *Growing up in Colonial America*. Brookfield, CT: Millbrook Press, 1995.

Berry, Erick. *Sybil Ludington's Ride*. New York: Viking Press, 1952.

Blake, William J. *The History of Putnam County, New York*. New York: Baker & Scribner, 1849.

Brown, Drollene P. *Sybil Rides for Independence*. Niles, IL: Albert Whitman and Company, 1985.

Dacquino, V.T. *Sybil Ludington: The Call to Arms*. Fleishchmanns, NY: Purple Mountain Press, 2000.

Johnson, Willis Fletcher. *Colonel Henry Ludington: A Memoir*. New York: privately published by Charles and Lavinia Elizabeth Ludington, 1907.

Jones, Mary Elizabeth. *The Midnight Ride of Sybil Ludington and The Mystery of the Statue of King George III and His Horse*. Wilton, CT: Pimpewaug Press, 1976.

Mohr, Merilyn. *The Art of Soap Making*. Camden East, Ontario: Camden House Publishing, 1979.

Pelletreau, William S. *History of Putnam County, New York*. Philadelphia: W.W. Preston & Co., 1886.

Reed, Ethel. *Pioneer Kitchen: A Frontier Cookbook*. San Diego, CA: Frontier Heritage Press, 1971.

Index

Boston: 47
British:
    (army/soldiers/troops: 6, 7, 23, 24, 34, 46,
    47), (king: 3, 15), (rule: 2, 3, 7), (tax: 7)
Carmel: 31, 48, 49
Committee on Conspiracies: 2
Concord, Massachusetts: 47
Connecticut: 23
Continental Army: 1, 5, 24, 28, 46
Cooper, James Fenimore: 5
Crosby, Enoch: 3–5, 20
Danbury: 18, 22–25, 27–29, 34, 38, 40,
    44–47
Daughters of the American Revolution: 49
Duer, William: 2
Dutchess County: 47
English:
    (Parliament: 7), (guineas: 7)
Fort Riley: 49
Fredericksburgh: 2, 3, 7
Gallant Seventeen: 23
Hasbrouck family/farm: 13–17, 19, 20, 22,
    31, 32, 39–43
Huntington, Anna Leah: 49
Kansas: 49
keeping room: 10, 21, 27, 31
Longfellow, Henry
    Wadsworth: 47
Ludington, Colonel Henry: 2, 3, 7–9, 11, 12,
    16, 17, 20, 22, 23, 25–33, 38, 43–47, 50
    (reward: 7, 8)
Ludington family:
    (Rebecca: 7, 8, 18–23), (Archie: 29, 30,
    44), (Abigail/mother: 3, 4, 6, 7, 9, 10, 12,
    18–21, 23, 26, 27, 29–33, 41, 42, 45)
Ludington mill: 32, 34, 38, 44
Mahopac: 31, 34, 48
militia: 3, 4, 7, 8, 25, 28, 37, 38, 43, 46
    (minutemen: 47)
maple syrup (making of): 9, 10
Massachusetts: 47
muskets: 7, 14, 23
New York: 2, 6, 8, 13, 23, 47–49
Ogden, Edmond: 48
Ogden, Edmond Augustus: 49
Ogden, Henry: 48, 49
Patterson Baptist Church: 50
"Paul Revere's Ride": 47
Pecksville: 32, 42

Provincial Congress
    (of the State of New York: 2)
    (for the Colony of New York: 8)
Putnam County: 50
Redcoats: 3, 4, 6, 15, 17, 18, 24, 28, 29, 47
Redding Corners: 13
Red Mills: 13, 28, 31, 35, 36
Revere, Paul: 47
Shaw's Pond: 31, 34
Skinners: 13–17, 30, 32, 35, 39, 42
soap making: 18–22
spies: 4
Star (horse): 1, 4, 5, 9–11, 29, 30, 32–37,
    39–40, 42–44
Stormville: 32, 42
Sybil statue: 48, 49
The Spy: 5
Tory/Tories (Loyalists): 3, 7–9, 24, 25, 31, 32, 36
Tryon, General William: 25, 46, 47
Westchester County: 47
yellow fever: 48